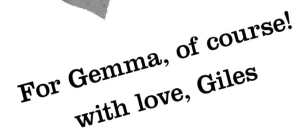
For Gemma, of course!
with love, Giles

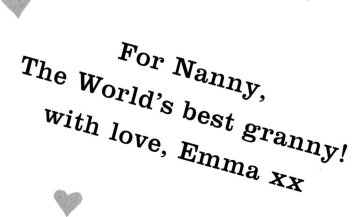
For Nanny,
The World's best granny!
with love, Emma xx

Text copyright © 2015 by Giles Andreae
Illustrations copyright © 2015 by Emma Dodd
First published in Great Britain in 2015 by Orchard Books, an imprint of
Hachette Children's Books

First US Edition, February 2017
10 9 8 7 6 5 4 3 2 1
F904-9088-1-15166

Printed in China

Library of Congress Cataloging-in-Publication Data
Andreae, Giles, 1966–
I love my grandma / Giles Andreae & Emma Dodd.—First edition.
pages cm
Summary: A celebration of the special bond between grandmother and grandchild.
ISBN 978-1-4847-3407-0—ISBN 1-4847-3407-6
[1. Stories in rhyme. 2. Grandmothers—Fiction.] I. Dodd, Emma, 1969- illustrator. II. Title.
PZ8.3.A54865Ian 2015
[E]—dc23   2015013106

Reinforced binding

Visit www.DisneyBooks.com

I love my grandma

Giles Andreae & Emma Dodd

Disney • HYPERION

Los Angeles   New York

I love my grandma. Can you tell?

She says I'm pretty great as well!

She's like a mom, but unlike mine,

she seems to have just loads of time.

I go 'round to her house to play,

And sometimes we just chat all day.

She knows a lot more things than me,

But then she's lived for ages, see?

She loves the photos Mommy sends,
And shows them off to all her friends.

She takes me out for special treats,
And sometimes buys us bags of sweets!

We ride on trains, and buses too,

and have adventures. Yes, we do!

We play all sorts of funny games,

And give each other silly names.

We really love to cook and bake,

And eat the yummy things we make.

We watch my favorites on TV,

And snuggle up, just her and me.

She's got a very comfy tummy.

"That," she says, "is very funny!"

And when it's time to say good-bye,

My grandma gives a little sigh . . .

And says, although we've had such fun . . .

. . . it's nice to give me

back to Mom.

I hope your grandma's just like mine.

We really have the bestest time!